Roger
Lancelyn Green

King Arthur's Court

D1136828

PENGUIN BOOKS

PENGUIN BOOKS

Published by the Penguin Group
Penguin Books Ltd, 27 Wrights Lane, London W8 5TZ, England
Penguin Books USA Inc., 375 Hudson Street, New York, New York 10014, USA
Penguin Books Australia Ltd, Ringwood, Victoria, Australia
Penguin Books Canada Ltd, 10 Alcorn Avenue, Toronto, Ontario, Canada M4V 3B2
Penguin Books (NZ) Ltd, 182–190 Wairau Road, Auckland 10, New Zealand

Penguin Books Ltd, Registered Offices: Harmondsworth, Middlesex, England

**First published in *King Arthur and his Knights of the Round Table*
in Puffin Books 1953**

This collection published in Penguin Books 1996
3 5 7 9 10 8 6 4 2

Set in 12.5/13pt Bembo Monotype
Typeset by Datix International Limited, Bungay, Suffolk
Printed in England by Clays Ltd, St Ives plc

Contents

The Two Swords

AFTER wicked King Vortigern had first invited the Saxons to settle in Britain and help him to fight the Picts and Scots, the land was never long at peace. Although so much of it was covered with thick forests, much also was beautiful open country, with little villages and towns, country houses and cottages, as the Romans had left it not many years before. Having once seen it, the Saxons could never again be contented with their savage, unfruitful homes in Germany and Denmark; and year by year more and more of them came stealing across the North Sea in their long ships, to kill or drive out the Britons and settle in their homes.

Vortigern was dead, and Aurelius Ambrosius, last of the Romans, was dead too, when Uther Pendragon, whom some call the brother of Ambrosius, led the Britons. He defeated the Saxons in many battles, and brought peace to the southern lands where he was king – to London, and to Winchester, which was then called Camelot, and to Cornwall where Gorlois his loyal follower was duke. But Uther fell in love 1 with Gorlois's wife, the lovely Igrayne, and there was battle between them, until Gorlois fell, and Uther married his widow.

He visited her first in the haunted castle of Tintagel, the dark castle by the Cornish sea, and Merlin the enchanter watched over their love. One child was born to Uther and Igrayne – but what became of that baby boy only the wise Merlin could have told, for he carried it away by a secret path down the cliff side in the dead of night, and no word was spoken of its fate.

Uther had no other children, though Igrayne and Gorlois had three daughters: two of these were grown-up when Igrayne became queen, and were married – Morgawse to Lot, King of Orkney, and Elaine to Nantres, King of Garlot: they had sons who in after days were among the bravest Knights of the Round Table. But the third daughter, Morgana le Fay, was still only a child, and she was sent to school in a nunnery; yet, by some means, she learnt much magic, which she used wickedly.

King Uther Pendragon had only a little while of happiness with the fair Igrayne, for soon the

Saxons made war against him once more, and

sent a traitor to serve him, who poisoned the King and many of his followers.

Then the land fell upon days more evil and wretched than any which had gone before. King Uther's knights fought amongst themselves, quarrelling as to who should rule; and the Saxons, seeing that there was no strong man to lead the Britons against them, conquered more and more of Britain.

Years of strife and misery went by, until the appointed time was at hand. Then Merlin, the good enchanter, came out from the deep, mysterious valleys of North Wales, which in those days was called Gwynedd, through Powys or South Wales, and passed on his way to London. And so great was his fame that neither Saxon nor Briton dared molest him.

Merlin came to London and spoke with the Archbishop; and a great gathering of knights was called for Christmas Day – so great that all of them could not find a place in the abbey church, so that some were forced to gather in the churchyard.

In the middle of the service, there arose suddenly a murmur of wonder outside the abbey: for there was seen, though no man saw it come, a great square slab of marble-stone in the 3 churchyard, and on the stone an anvil of iron, and set point downwards a great, shining sword of steel thrust deeply into the anvil.

'Stir not till the service be done,' commanded the Archbishop when this marvel was made known to him. 'But pray the more unto God that we may find a remedy for the sore wounds of our land.'

When the service was ended the Archbishop and the lords and knights who had been within the abbey came out to see the wonder of the sword. Round about the anvil they found letters of gold set in the great stone, and the letters read thus:

WHOSO PULLETH OUT THIS SWORD FROM THIS STONE AND ANVIL IS THE TRUE-BORN KING OF ALL BRITAIN.

When they saw this, many and many a man tried to pull out the sword – but not one of them could stir it a hair's breadth.

'He is not here,' said the Archbishop. 'But doubt not that God will send us our King. Let messengers be sent through all the land to tell what is written on the stone: and upon New Year's Day we will hold a great tournament, and see whether our King is amongst those who come to joust. Until then, I counsel that we appoint ten knights to guard the stone, and set a rich pavilion over it.'

All this was done, and upon New Year's Day a great host of knights met together. But none as yet could draw forth the sword out of the stone. Then they went all a little way off, and pitched tents, and held a tournament or sham-fight, trying their strength and skill at jousting with long lances of wood, or fighting with broad-swords.

It happened that among those who came was the good knight Sir Ector, and his son Kay, who had been made a knight not many months before; and with them came Arthur, Sir Kay's young brother, a youth of scarcely sixteen years of age.

Riding to the jousts, Sir Kay found suddenly that he had left his sword in his lodgings, and he asked Arthur to ride back and fetch it for him.

'Certainly I will,' said Arthur, who was always ready to do anything for other people, and back he rode to the town. But Sir Kay's mother had locked the door, and gone out to see the tournament, so that Arthur could not get into the lodgings at all.

This troubled Arthur very much. 'My brother Kay must have a sword,' he thought, as he rode 5 slowly back. 'It will be a shame and a matter for unkind jests if so young a knight comes to the jousts without a sword. But where can I find him one? . . . I know! I saw one sticking in an anvil in the churchyard, I'll fetch that: it's doing no good there!'

So Arthur set spurs to his horse and came to the churchyard. Tying his horse to the stile, he ran to the tent which had been set over the stone – and found that all ten of the guardian knights had also gone to the tournament. Without stopping to read what was written on the stone, Arthur pulled out the sword at a touch, ran back to his horse, and in a few minutes had caught up with Sir Kay and handed it over to him.

Arthur knew nothing of what sword it was, but Kay had already tried to pull it from the anvil, and saw at a glance that it was the same one. Instantly he rode to his father Sir Ector, and said:

'Sir! Look, here is the sword out of the stone! So you see I must be the true-born King of all Britain!'

But Sir Ector knew better than to believe Sir Kay too readily. Instead, he rode back with him 6 to the church, and there made him swear a solemn oath with his hands on the Bible to say truly how he came by the sword.

'My brother Arthur brought it to me,' said Kay, with a sigh.

'And how did *you* get the sword?' asked Sir Ector.

'Sir, I will tell you,' said Arthur, fearing that he had done wrong. 'Kay sent me to fetch his sword, but I could not come to it. Then I remembered having seen this sword sticking uselessly into an anvil in the churchyard. I thought it could be put to a better use in my brother's hand – so I fetched it.'

'Did you find no knights guarding the sword?' asked Sir Ector.

'Never a one,' said Arthur.

'Well, put the sword back into the anvil, and let us see you draw it out,' commanded Sir Ector.

'That's easily done,' said Arthur, puzzled by all this trouble over a sword, and he set it back easily into the anvil.

Then Sir Kay seized it by the hilt and pulled his hardest: but struggle and strain as he might, he could not move it by a hair's breadth. Sir Ector tried also, but with no better success. 7

'Pull it out,' he said to Arthur.

And Arthur, more and more bewildered, put his hand to the hilt and drew forth the sword as if out of a well-greased scabbard.

'Now,' said Sir Ector, kneeling before Arthur and bowing his head in reverence, 'I understand that you and none other are the true-born King of this land.'

'Why? Oh why is it I? Why do you kneel to me, my father?' cried Arthur.

'It is God's will that whoso might draw forth the sword out of the stone and out of the anvil is the true-born King of Britain,' said Sir Ector. 'Moreover, though I love you well, you are no son of mine. For Merlin brought you to me when you were a small child, and bade me bring you up as my own son!'

'Then if I am indeed King,' said Arthur, bowing his head over the cross-hilt of the sword, 'I hereby pledge myself to the service of God and of my people, to the righting of wrongs, to the driving-out of evil, to the bringing of peace and plenty to my land ... Good sir, you have been as a father to me since ever I can remember, be still near me with a father's love and a father's counsel and advice ... Kay, my foster-brother, be you seneschal over all my lands and a true knight of my court.'

After this they went to the Archbishop and told him all. But the knights and barons were filled with rage and jealousy, and refused to believe that Arthur was the true-born King. So the choice was put off until Easter; and at Easter once more until Whitsun, or Pentecost as it then was called: but still, though many kings and knights came to try their strength, Arthur alone could pull out the sword.

Then all the people cried: 'Arthur! We will have Arthur! By God's will he is our King! God save King Arthur!' And they knelt down before him, the noble and the humble together, the rich and the poor, and cried him mercy for delaying him so long. And Arthur forgave them readily, and kneeling down himself he gave the wondrous sword to the Archbishop and received of him the high and holy order of Knighthood. And then came all the earls and the barons, the knights and squires, and did homage to Arthur, swearing to serve and obey him as was their duty.

King Arthur now gathered together all the hosts of Britain, and with the pick of the older 9 knights who had served his father and the younger knights whose chief desire was to show their courage and loyalty, he set out to do battle with the Saxons and to punish all those thieves and robbers who had ravaged the land for many years, doing cruel and shameful deeds.

Before long he had brought peace and safety to the southern parts of Britain, making his capital at Camelot. But the other kings who ruled then in and about Britain – the Kings of Orkney and Lothian, of Gwynydd and Powys, of Gorre and Garloth – grew jealous of this unknown boy who was calling himself King of all Britain, and sent word that they were coming to visit him with gifts – but that their gifts would be given with sharp swords between the head and shoulders.

Then Merlin came suddenly to Arthur and led him to the city of Caerleon in South Wales, into a strong tower well provisioned for a siege. The hostile kings came also to Caerleon and surrounded the tower: but they could not break in, to kill Arthur and his faithful followers.

Merlin came out of the tower after fifteen
10 days, stood upon the steps in the gateway and

asked all the angry kings and knights why they came in arms against King Arthur.

'Why have you made that boy, that Arthur, our King?' they shouted.

'Be silent and listen, all of you!' commanded Merlin, and a great quiet fell upon all who were gathered together, an awe and a wonder as the good enchanter spoke to them.

'I will tell you of wondrous things,' he said. 'Arthur is indeed your King, the rightful King of all this land – yes, and of Wales too, of Ireland and Scotland and Orkney also, and of Armorica beyond the sea; and he shall rule other lands also. He is the true and only son of the good King Uther Pendragon! Of his birth and of the things which should befall when he was King, I knew by my holy arts. Uther came to Tintagel in the form of Gorlois three hours after Gorlois was dead: then and thus he comforted the Lady Igrayne and won her to be his wife. But, so my knowledge told me, their son, this Arthur, was born to great and wondrous things. A little while after his birth at dark Tintagel, Uther, who hearkened to my words, gave the child into my care, and I bore him to Avalon, the Land of Mystery. And the Dwellers 11 in Avalon – you know them not, but you would call them Fairies and Elves – cast a pure and great enchantment upon the child, a magic most strong. Three gifts they gave to Arthur: that he should be the best of all knights; that he should be the greatest king this land shall ever know; and that he should live long – longer than any man shall ever know. These, the virtues of a good and generous prince, the Dwellers in Avalon gave to Arthur. And in Avalon the elves are forging Excalibur to be the sword of his right – the clean flashing blade that shall be raised only in the cause of right, shining on the earth until the time comes when they shall call it back again . . . Arthur is your King! Year by year as he reigns, his kingdom shall grow – not Britain, nor the islands of the seas, no, nor Armorica and Gaul, – but Logres, the land of blessing, God's Kingdom upon earth, which Arthur shall show you for a little space before the darkness falls again.'

There was silence for a while when Merlin had finished speaking, for all those who heard him felt that they were at the beginning of a time of wonders, and that Arthur was more than 12 just a King who ruled because his father had been King, or because he was the strongest man amongst them.

Suddenly they all knelt before him where he stood above Merlin on the steps of the tower, and with one voice promised to be his true and faithful subjects all the days of their lives.

Then the Archbishop set the crown upon Arthur's head, and the people cheered him once more: and this was the real beginning of his reign.

'To-morrow we will begin to collect our forces,' said King Arthur. 'And when all are gathered together, we march to the north and to the east to do battle with the Saxons and drive them out of Britain. Then we will build castles and set guards along the coast so that never again may they invade us: we will rebuild the churches which they have destroyed, and build new ones to the glory of God; and our knights shall ride about the country punishing all those who break the peace and do ill to any. And if any man or woman, be he or she the greatest or the least of my subjects, be in any trouble, or have complaint against any man, let them come to me, and never shall their sorrow go uncomforted and their wrong unrighted.'

King Arthur feasted that day in the great castle of Caerleon: but before ever the feast was ended there befell the first of the marvellous adventures that were to happen in the wonderland of Logres during his reign.

Suddenly into the courtyard there rode a young squire, leading another horse, across the saddle of which lay the body of a knight but newly slain.

'Vengeance, lord King!' cried the squire, when Arthur came from the hall to learn what this might mean. 'Give me vengeance! Here lies Sir Miles, dead upon his steed, as goodly a knight and as brave as any in the land. In the forest not many leagues from here King Pellinore has set up his pavilion beside the high road, by a well of fresh water, and he goes about to slay all knights that pass this way. Wherefore I pray you that my master be honourably buried, and that some knight ride out to avenge his death.'

There was a certain squire in Arthur's court, whose name was Gryflet, no older than Arthur himself, and now he fell on his knees before the King and begged him for all his service to make him a knight so that he might go out and fight with Pellinore.

'You are not old enough yet for such a battle,' said King Arthur, 'nor have you grown great enough in strength.'

'Yet, make me a knight!' begged Gryflet.

'My lord,' said Merlin quietly to Arthur, 'it were a great pity to lose Gryflet, for he would be a passing good man when he comes of age, and would be your faithful knight all his life . . . Pellinore is the strongest man in the world now bearing arms, and surely Gryflet will be slain if they come to sword strokes.'

King Arthur nodded, and turned again to his young squire: 'Gryflet,' he said, 'kneel, and I will make you a knight according to your wish.' And when this was done, he went on: 'And now, Sir Gryflet, since I have made you knight, surely you owe me a gift.'

'My Lord, whatever you shall ask is yours,' said Gryflet.

'Promise me then,' commanded Arthur, 'by your honour as a knight, that when you come upon King Pellinore by the well in the forest, you joust but with your spears and, on horseback or on foot, fight with him in no other wise.'

'That will I promise you,' said Gryflet; and 15

then he took his horse in great haste, snatched up his spear, slung his shield on his left arm, and went off in a cloud of dust until he came to the well-side in the forest. And there he saw a rich pavilion, and before it a horse ready saddled and bridled, and at the side a tree on which hung a shield painted in bright colours, and by it a great spear.

Sir Gryflet hit the shield with the butt of his own spear so hard that it came clattering to the ground, and King Pellinore came out of the pavilion – a tall strong man as fierce as a lion.

'Sir knight!' he cried, 'why smote you down my shield?'

'Sir, for that I would joust with you!' answered Gryflet.

'It were better that you did not,' said King Pellinore. 'You are but a new, young knight, and not so strong as I!'

'In spite of that, I will joust with you,' repeated Gryflet.

'Well, this is by no desire of mine,' said King Pellinore as he buckled on his armour, 'but let things fall as they must. Whose knight are you?'

16　　'Sir, I am one of King Arthur's court!' cried

Gryflet. And with that they rode away in either direction along the road, then turned their horses, set their spears in rest, and galloped at one another as hard as they could. Sir Gryflet's spear struck the shield of King Pellinore and broke all to pieces: but King Pellinore's spear went straight through Gryflet's shield, deep into his side, and there broke off short. And Sir Gryflet and his horse fell upon the ground.

King Pellinore came and bent over Sir Gryflet, who lay still where he had fallen, and unloosed his helmet. 'Well, this was a brave youth,' said Pellinore, 'and if he lives, will be a mighty knight.' Then he placed Gryflet across the saddle, and the horse galloped back to Caerleon with none to guide it.

Arthur was very wroth when he saw how badly hurt was Sir Gryflet, and at once he put on his own armour, closed the vizor of his helmet so that no one could see his face, and with spear in hand rode hard into the forest to be revenged upon King Pellinore.

But on his way he found three robbers attacking Merlin, and they seemed like to beat him to death with great clubs.

'Fly, churls!' cried Arthur, riding at them 17

furiously, and the three cowards turned and fled when they saw the knight charging at them.

'Ah, Merlin,' said Arthur, 'for all your wisdom and your magic, you would have been murdered in a few minutes if I had not come to your rescue!'

'Not so,' answered Merlin, smiling his mysterious smile. 'Easily could I have saved myself, had I willed it. It is you who draw near to your death – for you go towards it in your pride, if God does not aid you.'

But Arthur would not take heed of Merlin's wisdom, and rode fiercely on until he came to the rich pavilion by the well. And there sat King Pellinore upon his great war-horse, waiting for him.

'Sir knight!' cried Arthur, 'why stand you here, fighting and striking down all the knights who ride this way?'

'It is my custom to do so,' answered Pellinore sternly. 'And if any man would make me change my custom, let him try at his peril!'

'I will make you change it!' cried Arthur.

'And I will defend my custom,' replied Pellinore quietly.

Then they drew apart, and came riding together at full tilt, so hard that both spears shivered into little pieces as each hit the centre of the other's shield. Arthur would have drawn his sword then, but Pellinore said:

'Not so, let us run together with spears yet again.'

'So I would,' said Arthur, 'if I had another spear!'

'I have plenty,' answered Pellinore, and he shouted to his squire to bring two out of the pavilion.

Once more the two kings jousted together; and once more their spears broke into fragments without either of them being struck from his horse. A third time they jousted, and Arthur's spear broke, but King Pellinore's struck him so hard in the middle of the shield that horse and man fell to the earth.

But Arthur sprang to his feet in a great fury, drawing his sword and shouting defiance at Pellinore, who thereupon came down from his horse and drew his own sword. Then began a fierce battle, with many great strokes; they hacked and hewed at one another, cutting pieces off their shields and armour, and suffering each of them so many wounds that the trampled grass in front of the pavilion was stained with red. 19

They rested once, and then charged each other again: but their swords met together with so mighty a crash that Arthur's broke in two, leaving him with the useless hilt in his hand.

'Ah-ha!' cried King Pellinore. 'Now you are in my power, to slay or spare as I will! And I will kill you forthwith, unless you kneel and yield to me, confessing yourself to be a knight of little worth.'

'There are two ways with that,' cried Arthur, mad with shame and fury. 'Death is welcome when it comes; but to yield – never!' And with that he leapt in under Pellinore's sword, seized him round the waist and hurled him to the ground. They struggled there for a little while, but Pellinore was still the strongest, and presently he tore off Arthur's helmet and took up his sword to cut his head off also.

But Merlin came suddenly and laid his hand on Pellinore's shoulder: 'Knight,' he said, 'hold your hand and do not strike this stroke. For if you do the hope of Logres dies, and you put this land of Britain into the greatest ruin and desolation that ever a country suffered.'

'Who is it?' asked Pellinore.

'This is King Arthur!' said Merlin.

For a moment Pellinore was tempted to strike the blow: for he feared that if Arthur lived, he would never forgive him for what he had done. But Merlin smiled quietly, and placed his hand on Pellinore's head. And at once all the anger and fear went from his mind, and he sank back quietly against the tree beside the well of clear water, and passed into a deep sleep.

Merlin helped King Arthur, who was sorely wounded, to mount his horse, and led him away into the forest.

'Alas, Merlin, what have you done?' asked Arthur; for now he had put from him all the pride and wilfulness which had so nearly caused his death. 'You have killed this good knight by your magic — and I would rather have lost my kingdom than that one so brave and mighty should die thus.'

'Cease to trouble,' said Merlin. 'For all things work by the will of God and to the glory of Logres. He is more like to live than you are, for you are sorely wounded, and he does but sleep . . . I told you how mighty a fighter he was. This is King Pellinore who in time to come shall do you good service. And his sons, Sir Tor and Sir 21

Lamorak, shall be among the bravest of your knights.'

Then Merlin brought Arthur to a hermitage where lived a good old man who was a clever leech, or healer of wounds. And in three days he was nearly cured, and could ride once more and fight as strongly as ever.

'Alas,' said Arthur as they rode through the forest. 'Now I have no sword.'

'Let not that trouble you,' said Merlin. 'There was no virtue in the sword which is lost: it has served its purpose. But near here your own sword awaits you: it was made in Avalon by fairy craft, made for you alone until you must return it ere you journey to Avalon yourself. It is called Excalibur, and none may stand against its stroke: and with it you shall bring freedom and peace to Logres. This is the hour appointed when Excalibur shall be placed in your hand – for now you will grasp its hilt in all humility, and draw it only to defend the right.'

Deeper and deeper into the forest they went, and before long the hills rose on either side until they were riding through a narrow valley that wound through dark mountains. And at last they
22 came to a narrow pass in the rocks, and beyond

it, in a cup of the mountains, Arthur saw a strange lake. All around it the hills rose darkly and desolately, but the lake water was of the clearest, sunniest blue, and the shore was covered thickly in fresh green grass and flowers. Over the brow of a little rise beyond the lake, the mountains opened out into a great plain, and beyond it was water, half hidden in mist, and broken with many islands.

'This is the Lake of the Fairy Palace,' said Merlin, 'and beyond the lake, over the brow of the hill yonder, lies the plain of Camlann where the last battle shall be fought, and you shall fall beneath the stroke of the Evil Knight. And beyond the plain lies Avalon, hidden in the mist and the mysterious waters . . . Go down now and speak with the Lady of the Lake, while I wait for you here.'

Leaving his horse with Merlin, Arthur went down the steep path to the side of the magic lake. Standing on the shore, he looked out across the quiet blue water – and there in the very centre of the Lake he saw an arm clothed in white samite with a hand holding above the surface a wondrous sword with a golden hilt set with jewels, and a jewelled scabbard and belt.

And then Arthur saw a beautiful damsel dressed in pale blue silk with a golden girdle, who walked across the water until she stood before him on the shore.

'I am the Lady of the Lake,' she said, 'and I am come to tell you that your sword Excalibur awaits you yonder. Do you wish to take the sword and wear it at your side?'

'Damsel,' said Arthur, 'that is indeed my wish.'

'For long I have guarded the sword,' said the Lady of the Lake. 'Give me but a gift when I shall come to ask you for one, and the sword shall be yours.'

'By my faith,' answered Arthur, 'I swear to give you whatsoever gift you shall ask for.'

'Enter into this boat, then,' said the Lady of the Lake. And Arthur saw a barge floating on the water before him, into which he stepped. The Lady of the Lake stood on the shore behind him, but the barge moved across the water as if unseen hands drew it by the keel, until Arthur came beside the arm clothed in white samite. Leaning out, he took the sword and the scabbard: and at once the arm and the hand which had held it sank quietly out of sight beneath the blue waters.

Then the barge brought Arthur to the shore where the Lady of the Lake had stood: but now she was gone also. He tied the barge to a tree-root which curved over the waterside, and strode joyfully up the steep path to the pass, buckling the sword Excalibur to his side as he went.

Merlin awaited him with the horses, and together they rode away into the forest, and back by many winding paths until they drew near the river which lay between them and Caerleon, and came to the straight, paved road leading to the city.

'In a little while,' said Merlin, 'King Pellinore will come riding towards us. For he has ceased to do battle with all who pass through the forest, having seen a Questing Beast which he must follow now for many years.'

'Then I will fight with him once more,' cried Arthur. 'Now that I have so good a sword as Excalibur maybe I shall overcome and slay him!'

Merlin shook his head: 'Let him pass,' he said, 'for so I counsel you. He is a brave knight and a mighty, and in days to come he will do you good service, and he and his sons shall be among the bravest in your court.'

'I will do as you advise me,' said Arthur. But he looked upon the sword Excalibur, and sighed.

'Which like you better, the sword or the scabbard?' asked Merlin.

'I like the sword!' cried Arthur.

'Then are you the more unwise,' said Merlin gravely. 'The scabbard is worth ten such swords: for while you wear that magic scabbard you shall lose but little blood, however sorely you are wounded. Keep well that scabbard, and have good care of it after I am gone from you, for a certain wicked lady who is nearly related to you shall seek to steal both sword and scabbard.'

They rode on, and in a little while met King Pellinore – who rode past as if he had not seen them.

'I marvel,' said Arthur, 'that he did not even speak to us!'

'He saw you not,' answered Merlin 'for my magic was upon him. But had you striven to stay him in your pride, then he would have seen you well enough.'

Before long they came to Caerleon, and his knights welcomed Arthur joyfully. And when they heard of his adventures, they were surprised that he should thus have gone into danger alone.

But all the bravest and noblest of them rejoiced exceedingly that they had such a king, one who would risk his life in an adventure as other ordinary knights did.

Balyn and Balan

IN Caerleon King Arthur remained for many months, gathering his followers from all parts of the country, and preparing them for the great battles that were to come when they should go over all the island of Britain, and across the sea into Armorica, which we now call Brittany, to punish the cruel and wicked and drive out or bring to order the heathen Saxons.

And while he was still preparing for the war, King Ryon of North Wales, one of the proudest and cruellest of the enemies of Logres, sent a message to King Arthur. And this was the message: that Ryon had conquered eleven lesser kings and cut off their beards to make a border to his royal mantle; and he would spare King Arthur on condition that he sent his beard to make the twelfth on the mantle, as a token that Ryon should be his over-lord and his master. Otherwise, he would enter Arthur's lands to burn and slay, until he had by force not only Arthur's beard, but his head also.

'This is the most shameful and unrighteous
28 message that ever I received,' said King Arthur to

the messengers. 'Go back to Ryon the savage; tell him that I will come against him with all my knights and fight until *his* head is smitten off – unless he comes to do me homage. For I owe him none, who am by right king of all Britain, and by divine will the maker of the realm of Logres – in which realm there is no place for such a monster as this Ryon!'

The messengers went away, and before long news came that King Ryon was gathering together an army, and that bands of his wicked followers were already ravaging the lands of Arthur's true subjects, burning and slaying wherever they came.

But there were other powers of evil warring against Logres – powers of magic harder to guard against and to overcome than King Ryon or the Saxons.

As Arthur held court with his knights in the castle of Caerleon, there came one day a damsel bearing a message to him. And when she had delivered her message, she let the cloak fall from her shoulders, and all could see that a great sword was fastened to her side.

'Wherefore do you wear that sword, Lady?' asked Arthur. 'Such an instrument of war does not suit a fair damsel such as you.'

'Now that you have asked me,' replied the damsel, 'I may tell you. This sword I bear with me is a token of my sorrow. I may not be free from it until I find a knight – a passing good man in deed and thought, without wickedness or treachery or evil thinking – who is able to draw it from the scabbard. I have been to the Court of King Ryon, where I was told there were good knights, but none might achieve the sword.'

'A great marvel indeed,' said Arthur. 'Yet not so strange among the followers of Ryon. But now let one of my knights set his hand to the hilt of it.'

Then a brave knight took hold of the sword and pulled eagerly – but he could not draw it.

'There is no need to pull half so hard,' said the damsel. 'In the right man's hand it will come out at a touch. But he must be a gentle knight, well-born and without evil in his heart.'

One after another the knights tried to draw the sword, but in turn each of them failed.

'Alas!' sobbed the damsel, 'I had thought that in the Court of King Arthur I would have found one man true enough knight to draw forth my sword!'

30

'By my faith,' said Arthur, half angered at her words, 'here are knights as good as any in the world – but they are not fated to help you, which troubles me sorely.'

But it happened that a young knight named Balyn, whom no one thought much of, for he had lately been in prison for killing a cousin of King Arthur's, came into the hall while all this was going on.

'Fair damsel,' he said presently, 'I pray you, of your kindness, let me try also to draw the sword. I am but a poor knight of Northumberland, but strong and passionate. And maybe these humble garments hide a better man than they seem.'

'You speak wisely,' said the damsel. 'Therefore try your fortune also.'

Then Balyn took the sword by the girdle and sheath, and drew it out easily. And when he looked upon the keen, shining blade, he loved it so much that it seemed worth more than the most precious thing in the world.

Many of the knights murmured, being jealous of Balyn, but the damsel said: 'Certainly this is a passing good knight, the best in all this land – and many great and wondrous deeds shall he do 31

. . . But now, kind and courteous sir, I beg you to give me back my sword.'

'Not so,' answered Balyn. 'With this sword I shall never part!'

'You are not wise to keep it,' said the damsel, 'for with it you shall slay the best friend that you have and the man you love best in the world. And that sword shall be your own destruction . . . It is a magic weapon which the Lady of the Isle of Avalon gave to me.'

'I will take my chances of what may come,' replied Balyn. 'But this sword I will not give up!'

Then the damsel made many lamentations, and departed from the Court in sorrow. And while Balyn stood to one side looking at his sword and rejoicing in it, and as the other knights crowded together talking of what had happened, the Lady of the Lake came suddenly into the hall and stood before King Arthur.

'Sire!' she cried. 'I hold you to your word! When I gave you your own sword you promised to grant me a gift.'

'That is true,' said Arthur. 'Therefore ask what you will, and you shall have it, if it is in my power to give.'

32   'Well,' said the Lady of the Lake, 'give me the

head of this knight who but now drew the sword which the damsel brought. I had rather that you had cut off her head – but it is too late for that.'

'Truly,' answered King Arthur, troubled and surprised at her words, 'I cannot in honour grant you the life of either of them. Sir Balyn is my guest.'

'I will take nothing else!' cried the Lady of the Lake.

Now when Balyn heard this, a madness seemed to come over him: 'Evil woman,' he cried, 'you would have my head, would you? Rather, you shall now lose your own!' And there and then, in the presence of King Arthur, he sprang forward and cut off her head at a single stroke.

'Alas, for shame!' said King Arthur, while all his knights murmured with reproach and disgust. 'Why have you done this? You have disgraced me and all my Court, for this damsel came to visit me, and was a lady of high worth. Therefore I will never forgive you for this deed.'

'Sire,' answered Balyn, 'be not displeased with me – for this lady was the falsest living, who had brought many brave men to their death, and women also.'

33

'Whatever the cause,' said Arthur, 'you have done a wicked and a shameful thing. Go now from my court, and from the realm of Logres, for you are no true knight unless you may redeem your honour by some brave deed or long penance.'

Balyn went with speed, mounted his horse, and rode out of Caerleon. Beyond the gate he commanded his squire to leave him:

'Go home to Northumberland,' he said, 'and tell them what has chanced. I myself shall ride in search of King Ryon and slay him, or die in the attempt: for if I slay Ryon, then surely King Arthur will be my friend again.'

But in King Arthur's court there was great wrath and uproar. And in the midst of it a proud knight of Ireland, Sir Launceor, who was jealous of Balyn for winning the sword, asked leave of King Arthur to ride after him and seek vengeance for the ill deed which had been done.

'Do your best,' said Arthur, 'for I am much angered with Balyn. I would that we might wipe out the shame that has fallen upon Logres by reason of that cowardly blow.'

34　　Sir Launceor went from court with all the

haste he might, and it was not long before he overtook Balyn.

But meanwhile Merlin came suddenly to the King and said:

'Evil has come into Logres and greater shall follow. The damsel who brought the sword has set the seeds of great and terrible things. That sword she had, by false means, from the Lady of the Isle of Avalon – and in that sword dwells a curse which must be borne to the end that in after days a blessing may come upon Logres by that sword in the hand of Galahad, truest knight of Logres. But alas for Balyn, for the curse is upon him who would have been of the bravest and best of your knights. He goes to his death, and naught can save him . . . Yet I will follow and see what good I may bring to him.'

While this was happening, Sir Launceor had come up with Balyn, who was riding up into the hills of Wales.

'Stay awhile!' he shouted as soon as he might be heard, 'or I will make you stay, whether you mean to or not! The shield you carry before you shall not help you – for I am after you!'

'Maybe you would have done better to stay at 35

home,' said Balyn, turning to meet him. 'Whence come you, and for what reason?'

'I am from the court of King Arthur,' answered Launceor. 'And I come to punish you for the evil stroke that you struck this day in his presence.'

'It grieves me much to have offended the best of kings,' said Balyn. 'But that damsel whom I slew was the wickedest in the world.'

'Make you ready, base knight!' was all that Launceor would reply. So the two of them fought there upon the hillside; and the end of it was that Balyn smote Sir Launceor through the body so that he fell to the ground dead.

Balyn stood beside him and was filled with sorrow at the death of a brave knight. But greater sorrow was to follow: for as he stood, a lovely maiden on a white horse came riding full speed up the hill. When she saw Launceor lie bleeding on the road, she cried aloud in great sorrow, and came and flung herself on the ground beside him.

'Ah, Balyn!' she sobbed. 'A sad stroke have you stricken! You have slain two bodies with one heart, and two hearts in one body, and two souls are lost by it!'

Then she took up Balyn's sword, which lay on the ground, and before he could stop her, flung herself upon the point of it and fell dead across the body of Sir Launceor whom she had loved better than life.

If Balyn was sad before, he was doubly sad now that he had caused the death of two such true lovers. And he would not be comforted, even when his brother Balan found him there – Balan whom he loved better than any in the world.

'Many sad things have indeed befallen you,' said Balan, 'but we must endure even the hardest adventures that God sends us.'

'That is so,' said Balyn. 'And now let us ride on, for I would find and slay the wicked Ryon of North Wales so that King Arthur may pardon me for the death of the Lady of the Lake.'

'I will come also,' said Balan, 'and put my body in adventure with you, as a brother ought to do.'

Deeper and deeper into the hills they went, through thick forests and by gloomy passes – and on a sudden they met Merlin, but Merlin disguised so that they did not recognize him.

'Whither do you ride?' asked Merlin.

'We do not tell our business to strangers,' said the two knights, Balyn adding: 'But tell us who you are that ask it.'

'At this time I will not tell you,' replied Merlin.

'That is an evil sign,' said Balyn. 'Surely you are no true man if you will not tell us your name.' And he put his hand to his sword.

'But I will tell you your name,' answered Merlin quietly. 'You are Balyn, the Knight of the Sword, and this is Balan your brother. And you go now to meet with King Ryon . . . But your quest will be of little use unless you are advised by me.'

'Ah,' said Balyn, bowing reverently. 'You are Merlin! We will indeed be ruled by your wisdom.'

'Follow me,' said Merlin, 'and you shall do a knightly deed . . . But unknightly deeds have been done by the Knight of the Sword, yet good as well as evil shall come of them to Logres . . . Sir Launceor lies dead, and with him his beloved, the Lady Columba: King Mark of Cornwall has found them, and will build a fair tomb above their bodies. And in days to come the greatest 38 battle ever fought between two knights shall fall out just there – between Launcelot and Tristram, whom the land knows not yet – and King Mark shall find sorrow there also. But woe to you, Balyn, for you shall strike the Dolorous Stroke: yet for the healing of that stroke shall the Holy Grail come to Logres, and the good knight Sir Galahad shall achieve it: and thereafter shall the darkness fall once more upon Logres.'

These things which the good enchanter told to them filled Balyn and Balan with awe and wonder, and they rode on in silence until the fall of night.

'Dismount now,' said Merlin, 'unbridle your horses, leave them and follow me.'

In the midst of a dark wood they came to a little glade filled with soft moonlight.

'Abide hereby,' said Merlin, 'for at midnight King Ryon comes here secretly with but a few men to take by force the Lady of Vaunce who is to pass this way with two knights, in search of her lord.'

King Ryon came with twenty armed men, and Balyn and Balan attacked them with such fury that many were slain and the rest fled. But King Ryon turned to fight with Balyn, and after a great battle he fell wounded to the ground. 39

'Brave knights,' said Ryon, 'I pray you, slay me not. You may gain much by my life, but little by my death.'

'You speak truth,' said Balyn. 'You shall come yet living to King Arthur.'

'I will lead him to Caerleon,' said Merlin, 'for here you must abide till the great battle that is to be, when you shall do King Arthur good service.'

Merlin came to Caerleon as Arthur was about to march into North Wales. 'I bring you your worst enemy,' he said. 'But he was overcome and taken by two good knights whom you shall know at the great battle you go now to fight. It shall be before the walls of Castle Tarabil, and there you shall conquer twelve kings.'

King Arthur marched onward, and the twelve kings made ready for him. King Ryon was with them no longer, but Lot of Orkney had been persuaded by evil counsel to join them, which was a sad thing, for he was a brave man and a good and noble king, and the husband of Morgawse, Arthur's half-sister.

All through one long day the battle of Castle 40 Tarabil was fought, and for long it seemed that

Arthur must lose. But on a sudden two knights came riding out of the forest and entered the battle from behind, striking such blows and fighting so furiously, that the twelve kings thought that a new army was come against them, and broke and fled.

In the evening only King Lot remained alive of the twelve kings, and only his followers still fought on – for none could overcome King Lot. Then on a sudden came King Pellinore, following the Questing Beast across the world as his fate was, and he fought with Lot, and struck him such a mighty blow with his sword that Lot fell to the ground and died, and the hosts of Orkney fled into the darkness.

'You have won a great battle for Logres,' said Merlin, 'but the victory belongs to the Knight of the Sword and his brother, and to the Knight of the Questing Beast.'

'And who are these?' asked Arthur. 'King Pellinore I know, but not the others.'

'It is Balyn, who drew the damsel's sword,' said Merlin, 'and Balan his brother. Balyn you will meet once again, but Balan never. They shall die both on the same day, a sorrowful, unholy death. The tale of Balyn and Balan shall be the saddest 41 of any, for he who drew that sword is the most unfortunate of all knights.'

'Alas,' said King Arthur, 'that is a pity indeed, for I owe him much gratitude for his deeds this day – and I have little deserved what he has done for me.'

After the battle Arthur marched on through the great forests which covered so much of Britain in those days, to make war against the Saxons in the north. And one day when they had pitched camp in the forest and King Arthur was resting in his pavilion in an open glade near by, he heard the sound of a horse's hooves, and looking out he saw a knight ride slowly by who sighed and lamented loudly as if some dreadful ill had befallen him.

'Stay a while, fair sir!' cried Arthur, 'and tell me wherefore you sorrow thus.'

'You can do nothing to help me,' said the knight, and he rode sadly on his way.

A little while later came Balyn, and knelt to King Arthur. 'Now by my head!' said the King, 'you are right welcome.'

'I may not abide,' said Balyn, 'for a sore curse is upon me and evil will come upon all those 42 who are with me for long. But I pray you, my good lord king, give me some quest to follow, so that I may strive for the making of Logres before the evil overtakes me.'

'It grieves me that you cannot stay to follow me,' said King Arthur. 'But Merlin has told me of your fate. And as for a quest – but now a knight rode by, crying and lamenting some great sorrow. Wherefore I desire you to follow him and bring him to me that we may help him if any help is to be found in man.'

Balyn rode on as fast as he could, and before long found the knight riding beside a damsel in the forest. 'Sir knight!' he cried, 'you must turn round and come back with me to King Arthur to tell him the cause of your sorrow!'

'That I will not,' said the knight, 'for it will harm me greatly and do me no good.'

'Sir,' said Balyn, 'I pray you, make ready to obey me, for otherwise I will fight with you, and bring you by force.'

'Will you promise me safe-conduct if I come?' said the knight. 'There is much evil abroad in this forest – yet from black enchantment I cannot fly.'

'Surely I will give you safety,' said Balyn, 'or else die for it!'

They rode back after this, the damsel waiting in the forest, until they came to the king's pavilion. But there, right in front of it, in the very presence of King Arthur, there came one invisible and smote the knight who rode with Balyn through the body with a spear.

'Alas!' said the knight, 'even under your safe-conduct am I slain. That was the false knight Garlon who, by black magic, rides invisible. The evil has come upon me as I feared it would. But mount now my horse, which is faster than your own, ride back to the damsel in the forest and follow the quest that I was on as she will lead you, till you have avenged my death.'

Then the knight fell dead to the ground, and in great sorrow Balyn mounted his horse and rode to the damsel, whom he told of all that had happened.

Together they rode on towards the Castle of Meliot, but before they reached it they overtook another knight who was returning from hunting. They rode with him on his way, but in a little came Garlon the invisible knight and smote him as well, so that he fell down and died.

'For this also shall I do vengeance upon Garlon the coward and traitor,' said Balyn; and they came to the gateway of Castle Meliot. Balyn strode first over the drawbridge into the castle, with the damsel behind him: but as soon as he had passed under the gateway, the portcullis was let down, so that there was a grating of iron and wood between him and the damsel.

Then many men ran together and took the damsel, and it seemed to Balyn that they were about to kill her. He could not break through the portcullis, but instead he ran up the nearest stairway and jumped twenty feet from a window into the dry moat, and fell upon the men with drawn sword.

'Fair knight,' said the leader of them, 'we will not fight with you, nor would we do harm to you or to the damsel. But the lady of this castle has lain sick this many a year, and the custom of the land is that all damsels who pass this way must seek to heal her, which may be done with the blood of a pure maid of noble birth – and the maid shall not suffer therefrom.'

'Well,' said Balyn, 'if the damsel wills it, you may take blood from her: but do her no harm, for I would not for my life that any ill should befall her.'

Then they came within the castle, and the 45

damsel gave of her blood in a silver dish: but it did not heal the lady, for only the sister of the pure knight Sir Percivale could do that when, in days to come, she and her brother should pass that way in quest of the Holy Grail.

After this, the Knight of Meliot, who was lord of the castle, made Balyn and the damsel welcome to a good feast and comfortable lodgings. But as they sat at supper, Balyn heard in the next room the sound of a man groaning as if in great pain.

'What is that noise?' he asked.

'But a little while ago,' said the Knight of Meliot, 'I jousted at Castle Carbonek, and twice I smote down a knight of King Pelles' following. Then this villain knight swore to be revenged by hurting the one I loved best; and the next day he rode invisible and smote my son, who may not now be healed of his grievous wound until I have that knight's blood – whose name ever I know not.'

'Ah,' said Balyn, 'that knight is Garlon, who has slain two knights in like manner: indeed I am now in quest of him that I may slay him to avenge the wrong he has done to this damsel.'

46 'I will tell you how to find him!' cried the

Knight of Meliot. 'King Pelles will shortly hold a great feast in Castle Carbonek to which any knight may come, but each must bring with him his chosen damsel. And there you shall find this Garlon – your enemy and mine.'

The very next morning they set out, and in fifteen days came to Castle Carbonek and were welcomed to the feast. But the Knight of Meliot was made to remain outside, since he had brought no lady with him.

Balyn was led to a fair chamber where he was unarmed and clothed in rich robes. Now his sword was taken from him, for the custom was that no man might come armed to the feast: but Balyn hid his own long dagger beneath his robe, and so came down with his damsel into the great hall where the other knights and ladies were gathered.

Presently Balyn asked: 'Is there not a knight in this court whose name is Garlon?'

'Over there you may see him,' he was told, 'the knight with the cruel, dark face. But indeed he is the most marvellous man now living, for he can ride invisible and slay whomsoever he will.'

'Indeed,' said Balyn, 'so that is Garlon.' And then he thought to himself: 'If I kill him here where all these knights and ladies may see, I shall not escape with my life; but if I leave him now, I may never find him again – and he will do much harm if he lives.'

Now as he sat looking at him and wondering what to do, Garlon saw him, and coming over, struck him in the face, saying: 'Knight, why do you stare at me like this? For shame! Eat your meat, and do what you came for!'

'It were shame indeed not to avenge this insult – and all the other ill deeds which you have done,' cried Balyn springing up. 'And as to what I came for – it was to do this!' And as he spoke, he drew his dagger and stabbed Garlon to the heart, so that he fell down dead.

Then there was a great commotion in the hall. 'Sir, wherefore have you slain Garlon who was my guest?' cried King Pelles. 'For this evil deed, surely you shall be slain before you depart from the Castle of Carbonek!'

'Well,' cried Balyn, 'come and kill me if you dare!'

'Yes,' said King Pelles, 'no man shall do it but I, for Garlon was my knight.' And as he said this, King Pelles snatched a great sword from the wall 48 and struck fiercely at Balyn, who guarded the blow from his head with the long dagger. But so mighty a stroke had King Pelles stricken, that Balyn's dagger flew into small pieces.

When Balyn found that he was weaponless, he turned and ran, seeking for a sword or a spear with which to fight; and King Pelles followed him, still in a great rage.

Away went Balyn out of the hall with King Pelles behind him, along stone passages, up dark spiral staircases, and through room after room of that great, mysterious castle. And at last he came to a great tower far away from the part where anyone lived, or had lived for many centuries: and still up and up the tower he went, until, near the top, he paused at a closed door, and a great feeling of awe and fear began to creep over him. But he heard King Pelles clattering up the stone steps behind him, so he pushed open the door and sprang into the room.

As Balyn stepped across the threshold a Voice said to him: 'Enter not into this room, for you are unworthy!' But there was no one in the room.

Balyn looked about him, and saw a table made of silver standing in an alcove under an archway of the most beautiful carved marble; the table 49 was spread with a fair white cloth which showed no sign of dust or age, and on it stood a great cup under a silken cloth – and it seemed to Balyn that the cup was filled with light, so that he could hardly bear to look at it.

He was trembling now, he did not know why, and he seemed to wish nothing so much as to kneel before that table and the cup upon it and pray for the blessing of God. But he saw above the table a strange spear which hung point downwards with nothing to support it: and once more he heard King Pelles behind him, stumbling over the threshold of the room.

Then Balyn leapt forward to seize the spear: 'Sinner, touch it not!' cried the Voice again. But he did not heed it, for now he seemed to wish for nothing but to turn and slay King Pelles.

King Pelles stood in the doorway, and he had dropped his weapon and all the hate had gone from him. But Balyn, in his madness, took the spear and struck the Dolorous Stroke, wounding King Pelles deeply in the side.

Then the Castle of Carbonek shook and rocked: all became dark, and a great wind seemed to seize Balyn and whirl him about and cast him bleeding and senseless on the ground, while a terrible cry of woe rang in his ears and went echoing away across the distance.

Three days Balyn lay senseless among the ruins which alone remained of much of the castle; and on the fourth Merlin came, and drew him out, and set him upon a horse.

'Sir, I would have my damsel,' said Balyn feebly, as he came to himself again.

'See,' answered Merlin, 'where she lies dead, and many another with her. You have struck the Dolorous Stroke and laid waste three counties. For the cup you saw was the Holy Grail wherefrom our blessed Lord Jesus Christ drank the wine at the Last Supper; and the spear which you laid impious hands upon, once pierced His side as He hung upon the Cross for all our sins. Now Pelles the maimed king lies wounded with a wound unhealable in the hall of Castle Carbonek, until Galahad the pure knight shall come to cure him after many years . . . Joseph of Arimathea, in whose tomb Our Lord was laid ere He rose again, brought them to Britain and died yonder in Castle Carbonek. The spear has accomplished the evil that must fall upon Logres, but the Grail awaits the truest holiness and purity wherewith Logres shall be blessed for a 51 little while before the end . . . But ride on now, for your fate calls you . . . And my own fate draws near also.'

Sad at heart, Balyn rode forward through the Waste Lands, and as he passed the people cried to him: 'Ah Balyn, you have brought great sorrow upon this country: doubt not but that vengeance shall fall upon you!'

At last he came out of those desolate fields and villages into the deep forests, and rode through them eight days until he came to a castle set on the bank of a fair, broad river. And as he came out of the forest, he heard a hunting-horn blow the *mort* – which is the call blown ever at the death of a deer.

'That blast,' said Balyn, 'is blown for me; for I am the prize, and yet I am not dead.'

A long bridge led across the river to the castle; and as Balyn drew near, a great company came riding across it to meet him: a hundred maidens singing more sweetly than the plaintive nightingale, and a hundred knights richly dressed riding gravely behind them.

The Lady of the Castle came to Balyn and said:

'Sir Knight, welcome are you to my castle:

here you may rest in peace after your toils and sorrows. But first, for so the custom is, you must fight with the Knight of the River, for he is our champion who dwells upon the island in midstream, and all who enter the castle must pass him.'

'It is a bad custom,' said Balyn, 'that a knight may not pass this way without doing battle with a stranger.'

'You need but this one battle,' said the Lady.

'Well,' answered Balyn, 'since I must fight, I am ready now. My horse is still fresh, though my heart is weary and I long to sleep.'

'Noble Sir,' said a knight to Balyn, 'I think that your shield is too small for such a battle: use mine, I beg you.'

Balyn thanked the knight, took his shield and rode down towards the river, looking to his armour as he went to see that he was well prepared for the fight.

As he came to the ford of the river, a damsel leant over the side of the bridge nearby and said:

'Oh! knight Balyn, why have you left your own shield? Alas, you have put yourself in greater danger yet, for by the painting on your 53 shield you would have been known. Alas, of all knights surely you are the most unfortunate!'

'I am sorry that ever I came within this country,' said Balyn, 'but I may not turn back now, or all would think that I was afraid.'

He came to the island, and there was a knight in black armour waiting for him, with vizor closed and no coat-of-arms upon his shield.

In silence they set their spears in rest, and rode at one another so hard that their spears were shattered and each flung from his horse so hard that they lay insensible for a few minutes. But soon they were on their feet again and fighting fiercely with their swords. First Balyn smote the Black Knight with his unhappy sword, so that the blood ran down to the ground; and then he was himself smitten until he fell.

As he rose to fight on, Balyn saw that the bridge and the castle walls were crowded with fair knights and sweet ladies who watched there in silence while the battle was fought. To it again they went, striking great strokes that might each have killed a weaker man: on and on until much of their armour was smitten away, and each was wounded with seven cruel wounds from which 54 the life-blood ran down on to the grass.

And at last the Black Knight sank to the ground, unable longer to stand on his feet. Balyn stood leaning on his sword, but without it he too would have fallen.

'What knight are you?' he asked hoarsely. 'For never till this day did I meet with one so brave, except only my brother.'

'My name,' said the Black Knight, 'is Balan, brother to the good knight Balyn!'

'Alas that ever I should have lived to see this day!' cried Balyn, and he fell to the ground in a swoon for loss of blood and in horror of what had chanced. Very slowly and painfully, crawling on his hands and knees, Balan drew near to Balyn, unlaced his helmet and looked upon his face. And Balyn awoke and cried:

'Oh Balan, my brother whom I love better than any man in the world, you have slain me, and I have slain you also – and men shall speak in sorrow of our deaths for evermore!'

'Alas that ever this should be!' sobbed Balan. 'Had you but carried your own shield, I would have known you by the arms upon it! And had I not overcome and slain the knight who kept this island in past times, I would not now have been its keeper armed all in black.'

Then the Lady of the Castle and her followers came to them, and Balan said: 'Lady, the same mother bore us who now die in the same hour, slain each by the other unknowing whom we struck. Bury us, I pray you, in the same tomb, and write upon it that here lie two brothers who slew one another by mischance, so that all who pass by may pray for our souls.'

Then Balan died, and Balyn a little later, and the Lady of the Castle caused their tomb to be made there upon the island in the river. And she set Balan's name upon the tomb, but his brother's she did not know.

When this was done, Merlin came suddenly to the place, and bade them write the name of Balyn, and that he was the unhappy knight who struck the Dolorous Stroke. Then he took the unlucky sword which had been broken in the fight, and set a new blade in the hilt, and laughed softly as he did so.

'Why do you laugh?' asked the Lady of the Castle.

'For this cause,' said Merlin. 'No man shall handle this sword now, save only Launcelot, and Galahad his son. And that shall be when the 56 knights of Logres seek for the Holy Grail . . . In the castle, also, you have a bed: but none shall lie in it without going mad, save Launcelot alone . . . But in the end Launcelot shall use this sword, and the bravest knight of Logres, the man he best loves in the world, shall fall beneath it. And that shall be Gawain . . . But soon thereafter shall come the last battle on the Plain of Camlann, and the darkness shall fall once more upon Logres.'

Merlin left the scabbard of Balyn's sword in the castle, where Galahad should find it. But the sword with the new blade he set with its point in a great stone which floated by magic upon the water: and no one knew whither it went until on the day appointed it should come to Camelot.

When all these things were done, Merlin came to King Arthur and told him of the Dolorous Stroke that Balyn had given King Pelles; and of how Balyn and Balan had fought and died upon the island in the river.

'Alas!' said King Arthur. 'This is the greatest pity that ever I heard tell of two knights. And two such knights as these I have as yet never known in Logres.'

PENGUIN CHILDREN'S 60s

ALI BABA AND THE FORTY THIEVES • *Retold by N. J. Dawood*
THE AMAZING PIPPI LONGSTOCKING • *Astrid Lindgren*
ANNE AT GREEN GABLES • *L. M. Montgomery*
AT THE RIVER-GATES
AND OTHER SUPERNATURAL STORIES • *Philippa Pearce*
CLASSIC GHOST STORIES
CLASSIC NONSENSE VERSE
THE CLOCKWORK MOUSE • *Dick King-Smith*
DEAD MAN'S LANE • *Joan Aiken*
THE DRAGON ON THE ROOF • *Terry Jones*
FOUR GREAT GREEK MYTHS • *Roger Lancelyn Green*
THE GREAT MOUSE PLOT AND
OTHER TALES OF CHILDHOOD • *Roald Dahl*
THE GREAT TIME WARP ADVENTURE • *Jon Scieszka*
THE HOOLIGAN'S SHAMPOO • *Philip Ridley*
KEEP IT IN THE FAMILY • *Anne Fine*
KING ARTHUR'S COURT • *Roger Lancelyn Green*
THE LITTLE MERMAID AND
OTHER FAIRY TALES • *Hans Andersen (Translated by Naomi Lewis)*
LOST DOG AND OTHER STORIES • *Penelope Lively*
THE MIDNIGHT STORY • *Margaret Mahy*
MOOMINTROLLS AND FRIENDS • *Tove Jansson*
MRS PEPPERPOT TURNS DETECTIVE • *Alf Prøysen*
THE NIGHT TRAIN: STORIES IN PROSE AND VERSE • *Allan Ahlberg*
THE PIED PIPER OF HAMELIN AND OTHER CLASSIC STORIES IN VERSE
ROBIN HOOD AND HIS MERRY MEN • *Roger Lancelyn Green*
SHERLOCK HOLMES AND THE SPECKLED BAND • *Sir Arthur Conan Doyle*
SMACKING MY LIPS • *Michael Rosen*
TALES FROM ALICE IN WONDERLAND • *Lewis Carroll*
TALES FROM THE JUNGLE BOOK • *Rudyard Kipling*
THREE QUIRKY TAILS • *Paul Jennings*
TOM SAWYER'S PIRATE ADVENTURE • *Mark Twain*
TOM THUMB AND OTHER FAIRY TALES • *Jacob and Wilhelm Grimm*

Some Puffin books by Roger Lancelyn Green

THE ADVENTURES OF ROBIN HOOD
KING ARTHUR AND HIS KNIGHTS OF THE
ROUND TABLE
THE LUCK OF TROY
MYTHS OF THE NORSEMEN
THE TALE OF TROY
TALES OF ANCIENT EGYPT
TALES OF THE GREEK HEROES